Construction Zone

Building a Skyscraper

by JoAnn Early Macken

Consulting Editor: Gail Saunders-Smith, PhD

Consultant: Don Matson, owner
Metro Construction, Paving, and Excavating
Roseville, Minnesota

Capstone
press

Mankato, Minnesota

Pebble Plus is published by Capstone Press,
151 Good Counsel Drive, P.O. Box 669, Mankato, Minnesota 56002.
www.capstonepress.com

1 2 3 4 5 6 13 12 11 10 09 08

Library of Congress Cataloging-in-Publication Data
Macken, JoAnn Early, 1953–
    Building a skyscraper/by JoAnn Early Macken.
    p. cm. — (Pebble plus. Construction zone)
    Summary: "Simple text and photographs present the construction of a skyscraper, including information
on the workers and equipment needed"— Provided by publisher.
    Includes bibliographical references and index.
    ISBN-13: 978-1-4296-1233-3 (hardcover)
    ISBN-10: 1-4296-1233-9 (hardcover)
    1. Skyscrapers — Juvenile literature. I. Title. II. Series.
TH1615.M35 2008
720'.483 — dc22   2007027105

Editorial Credits
Sarah L. Schuette, editor; Patrick Dentinger, designer; Jo Miller, photo researcher

Photo Credits
Corbis/epa/Michael Reynolds, cover
Dreamstime/Elena Elisseeva, 1; Thorsten, 19; Tom Dowd, 21
Getty Images Inc./Asia Images/Tony Metaxas, 7; Photographer's Choice/David Oliver, 17
Shutterstock/Albert H. Teich, 11; Donald R. Swartz, 5; Goygel-Sokol Dmitry, 13; PhotoCreate, 15;
    Serg54, cover (sky); Stephen Finn, 9

Note to Parents and Teachers

The Construction Zone set supports national science standards related to understanding
science and technology. This book describes and illustrates building a skyscraper. The
images support early readers in understanding the text. The repetition of words and
phrases helps early readers learn new words. This book also introduces early readers to
subject-specific vocabulary words, which are defined in the Glossary section. Early
readers may need assistance to read some words and to use the Table of Contents,
Glossary, Read More, Internet Sites, and Index sections of the book.

Table of Contents

Skyscrapers

Large cities are filled
with tall skyscrapers.
Many people live
and work in skyscrapers.

Architects draw plans
for new skyscrapers.
They look for good places
to build.

Getting Ready

Workers clear the area.

Graders level the ground.

Pile drivers pound
deep holes.
Cranes lift steel bars
into the holes to make
the building's frame.

Construction

The skyscraper grows
from the bottom up.
Workers pour concrete
to make each story.

On the inside,
workers build walls.
Workers put in windows
and doors.

Electricians put in
wires and lights.
Workers add elevators
and stairs.

17

A New Skyscraper

Construction is finished.
The skyscraper seems
to touch the sky.

19

People can look out
over the city
in the new skyscraper.

Glossary

architect — a person who designs and draws plans for buildings, bridges, and other construction projects

concrete — a mixture of cement, water, sand, and gravel that hardens when it dries

frame — the base that a skyscraper is built around; steel frames give support and shape to tall buildings so they don't tip over.

pile driver — a machine that drives beams into the ground to hold up a building or bridge

steel — a hard metal made from iron

story — the floor of a building; skyscrapers have many stories.

Read More

Hyland, Tony. *High-Rise Workers.* Extreme Jobs. North Mankato, Minn.: Smart Apple Media, 2006.

Rau, Dana Meachen. *Skyscraper.* Bookworms: The Inside Story. New York: Marshall Cavendish Benchmark, 2007.

Williams, Linda D. *Cranes.* Pebble Plus. Mighty Machines. Mankato, Minn.: Capstone Press, 2005.

Internet Sites

FactHound offers a safe, fun way to find Internet sites related to this book. All of the sites on FactHound have been researched by our staff.

Here's how:

1. Visit *www.facthound.com*

2. Choose your grade level.

3. Type in this book ID **1429612339** for age-appropriate sites. You may also browse subjects by clicking on letters, or by clicking on pictures and words.

4. Click on the **Fetch It** button.

FactHound will fetch the best sites for you!

Index

Word Count: 110
Grade: 1
Early-Intervention Level: 18

24